TINY TREE
CHILDREN'S BOOKS

First Published 2018

Tiny Tree Children's Books (an imprint of Matthew James Publishing Ltd)

Unit 46, Goyt Mill

Marple

Stockport

SK6 7HX

www.tinytreebooks.com

ISBN: 978-1-910265-65-9

Illustrations by Howard Gray

Printed by Chapel Print Ltd

ROCHESTER | www.chapelprint.com

This is **Danny.**

Danny's dreams
danced with dogs.

He thought about what his
dream dog would look like.

He imagined all the
exciting things they would
do together.

But Mum always said he couldn't have a dog.

Danny tried **everything**.

He asked nicely.
He pleaded.
He whined.
He begged.

He played with his toy dogs. He took them for walks, fed them, brushed them. He even picked up pretend poo!

But mum *still* said no.

"It wouldn't be fair Danny," she explained. "I'm out at work all day and you're at school, so the poor thing would be left indoors on its own."

One day a new neighbour moved in below them.

And she brought her **dog** with her!

Mum had a cup of tea with their new neighbour, "My knees mean I can't walk **Maximus** at the moment," Mrs. Owen sighed. "Not going out makes him very miserable."

Mum told Danny about Maximus. "He needs to go for a walk every day," she said. "So I told Mrs. Owen you love dogs and promised you would take Maximus out, starting tomorrow."

Mon – Walk Max
Tues – Walk Max
Wed – Walk Max
Thur – Walk
Fri – Walk
Sat – Wal
Sun – Wal

Danny was so excited! It was going to be **amazing!** He couldn't wait to meet Maximus. When he fell asleep that night his dreams were filled with the fun he was going to have the next day.

When school was over, Danny
rushed home to meet Maximus
for the first time.

He didn't look like Danny's
idea of a dream dog.

He didn't **behave** like one either!

But a promise is a promise.
Danny walked Maximus every day.

At first, Maximus was so excited
to be out that he pulled on his
lead and would not do anything
that Danny told him to.

On rainy days it was really
miserable, and Maximus became
a bit stinky when he got wet.

Maximus was especially enthusiastic about rabbits.

And **squirrels**.

And other dogs.

And briefcases, particularly ones with sausage sandwiches in them.

Max quickly got to know **everyone** in the park.

Despite the drizzle
and the drama, Danny
began to look forward
to seeing Max at the
end of each day.

Max was always pleased to see Danny. He began to behave himself. Well, most of the time anyway!

When he got back from his walks, Danny shared a drink and a biscuit with Mrs. Owen. He told her about the day's adventures.

Before long, Danny found he was not dreaming about dogs anymore. He loved Max, even though he was small, scruffy, naughty and sometimes a bit smelly.

In the end, Danny decided it was much nicer to have a share in a real dog rather than a whole imaginary one.

Mum was happy.

Danny was happy.

Max was happy.

Mrs. Owen
was happy.

Max, as it turns out, was everyone's dream dog.

Danny helps Mrs. Owen look after Maximus.

There are lots of people out there who might need help caring for their pet.

The Cinnamon Trust is an amazing charity for people in their last years and their much loved, much needed companion animals.

A network of 15,000 volunteers "hold hands" with owners to provide vital loving care for their pets. Volunteers keep owners and pets together. That might mean walking a dog every day for a housebound owner, fostering pets when owners need hospital care, fetching the pet food or even cleaning out the bird cage.

When staying at home is no longer an option, the Trust maintains a register of care homes and retirement housing happy to accept residents with pets. Planning ahead with the Trust can also mean that they will take on life-time care of a bereaved pet.

In the year to March 2018, the trust helped **86,748** people with **108,435** pets.

www.cinnamon.org.uk

The Cinnamon Trust
10 Market Square, Hayle
Cornwall TR27 4HE
Charity Number 1134680